This book is to be returned on or before the last date stamped below.

2
2
1
10
1

KINGS FARM

CHARTER MARK
Awarded for excellence
to Arts & Libraries

2 9 DEC 2018

Kent
County
Council

D0183207

C153680906

"... on.
Lions are supposed to be brave
but I was a scaredy cat . . ."

Hana

Lee

MR BROWN

Betty

Owen

Francis

MRS LioN

BeRT

KENT
LIBRARIES & ARCHIVES
C153680906

LEE, THE LION WHO DIDN'T LIKE GOING TO THE DENTIST
A RED FOX BOOK 978 1 862 30577 9

First published in Great Britain by Red Fox,
an imprint of Random House Children's Books
A Random House Group Company

This edition published 2008

1 3 5 7 9 10 8 6 4 2

Text copyright © Red Fox, 2008
Hana's Helpline copyright © 2006 Calon Limited
Hana's Helpline is a registered trademark of Calon.

All rights reserved. No part of this publication may be reproduced, stored in a retrieval system,
or transmitted in any form or by any means, electronic, mechanical, photocopying,
recording or otherwise, without the prior permission of the publishers.

Red Fox Books are published by Random House Children's Books,
61–63 Uxbridge Road, London W5 5SA

www.kidsatrandomhouse.co.uk
www.rbooks.co.uk

Addresses for companies within The Random House Group Limited can be found at: www.randomhouse.co.uk/offices.htm

THE RANDOM HOUSE GROUP Limited Reg. No. 954009

A CIP catalogue record for this book is available from the British Library.

Printed in China

# Hana's Helpline

# Lee

# THE LION WHO DIDN'T LIKE GOING TO THE DENTIST

Lee was playing in the park with Bert, Ellen and Francis. He caught Bert and roared, "Caught you, Bert."

Bert looked at Lee's teeth. "Wow! What big teeth," he said.

"Yes, my mum's taking me to the dentist tomorrow. What's a dentist?" said Lee.

"A tooth doctor," said Bert wisely.

"My great-uncle Arthur went to the dentist, and he gave him teeth like this!" He pulled out some joke snapping teeth.

Lee looked at the teeth and ran away. He was really scared!

At Hana's Helpline, Betty and Hana were hard at work. Betty was looking for her sandwich. Had she filed it under 's' for sandwich? No, she'd filed it under 'd' for delicious!

"Ouch," she cried as she bit into it. "My tooth!"

"Are you OK, Betty?" asked Hana. "Maybe you should go to the dentist?"

That night Lee had an awful nightmare and dreamed that a giant pair of false teeth was chasing him through the park. When he woke up he was very scared. Then he saw the Hana's Helpline advert. "Maybe Hana can help me," he thought.

"Moo, Baa, Double Quack, Double Quack. Hana's Helpline," said Hana. Lee explained his problem to her.

"Well, poppet, some people are afraid of going to the dentist but there's no need to be," said Hana. "Why don't you go with your mum and see?"

Lee thought for a moment and then agreed.

"Now how about a nice cup of tea?" said Hana.
Betty bit into a cake. "Oooh!" she groaned.
"Right," said Hana, "you need
to go to the dentist, now!" Betty
nodded.

Mr Brown, the dentist, was very nice. "Now just relax, open your mouth wide and let's see what the problem is," he said to Betty.

He looked inside Betty's mouth. "Aah, I see," he said. "You need a small filling. You'll soon feel as good as new."

Mrs Lion had brought Lee along to see that the dentist wasn't frightening after all. He was playing happily with the toys when he heard a dreadful noise. Someone was yelling and screaming from inside the dentist's surgery! He ran away as quickly as he could.

On the way back home through the park Mrs Lion and Lee saw the other little animals playing.

"Hi, Lee," said Francis. "Mrs Lion, can Lee come and play?"

Lee was still scared. "No, I don't want to," he said.

"I'm sorry," said Mrs Lion. "Lee isn't quite himself. We went to the dentist but he got frightened and ran out."

"Bert, this is all your fault," said Francis.

"Why, what did I do?" asked Bert. Francis took out Bert's joke teeth. "Oh!" said Bert.

"Come on," said Francis. "We must try and put this right. Let's talk to Lee."

But Lee didn't want to talk or even see Bert and Francis. He wouldn't answer the door and he shut the curtains.

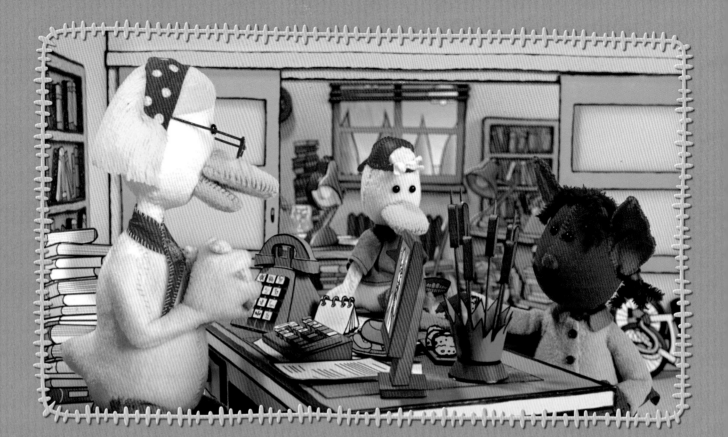

Betty was back from the dentist. "So how's your toothache?" asked Hana.

"Much better, thank you," said Betty. "It didn't hurt at all. In fact the only person who cried was Mr Brown. You see, what happened was . . ." Just then the phone rang!

"Hello, Lee," said Hana. "I'm glad you called." She listened as Lee told her about the screaming at the dentist's office. "I know, Lee," said Hana. "But that was poor Mr Brown — he tripped over Betty's bike and hurt himself. So will you show your mum what a brave little lion you can be and go back to the dentist?"

Lee and his mum went back to the dentist. Lee felt very brave. Poor Mr Brown had a bandage round his head after his fall over Betty's bike.

"Hello, Lee," said Mr Brown. "Come on in. There's nothing to be worried about."

Lee looked around nervously — he didn't know what anything was!

"There's nothing to be afraid of, Lee," said Mr Brown. "If you sit on this chair, I can have a good look at your teeth."

"Now say, 'Aaaah'," said Mr Brown.

"Aaaah," said Lee.

"Good boy," said Mr Brown. "All these teeth look very healthy. Do you clean them twice a day?"

Lee nodded. Mr Brown looked pleased.

"Well, Lee's teeth look fine," said Mr Brown to Mrs Lion. "You've been very good, Lee. Here is a sticker for being a brave lion."

Lee felt very brave and wasn't scared of going to the dentist any more!

# Hana's Help Point

## Hana's Tips For a Trip to the Dentist

If you are worried about going to the dentist, don't worry! Hana can help!

**Ask an adult to take you to the dentist to see what it is like.**

★ Try just playing in the waiting room if you don't want to see the dentist at first

★ Sometimes dentists have stickers and colouring!

**What to eat to keep your teeth healthy:**

fruit

vegetables

water

**What NOT to eat to keep your teeth healthy:**

fizzy drinks

chocolate

crisps

sweets

## How to brush your teeth:

★ Put a pea-sized blob of fluoride toothpaste onto your toothbrush

★ Make circular movements with your brush

★ Always start and end at the same point

## Time to play dentists!

★ You can pretend you're a dentist and brush your mummy or daddy's teeth for them!

★ Make sure your doll or teddy keep their teeth clean, too!

DON'T FORGET TO BRUSH YOUR TEETH!

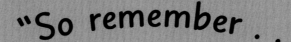

"So remember . . .

. . . if you're in trouble and you need help,
ring me, Hana, on **Moo, Baa,
Double Quack, Double Quack!**"